THE LAST ONE TO MURDER

ERIC REESE

ISBN: 978-1-925988-20-8

While seeking revenge, dig two graves - one
for yourself.

DOUGLAS HORTON

CONTENTS

Xuan Lang pulled his suitcase across the white tiles, staring at Airport Exit B. There were people rushing inside the terminal from the rain, while Xuan only wanted a taxi to his new address. Mr. Lang had arrived in the United States for six months and wasn't sure if he'd be finished his mission by his visa's expiration. He wondered if he'd be welcomed by the Americans since the Vietnam War five years ago had left deep scars and many false stereotypes.

His mission would require many hurdles. As Xuan pondered his plans during his ride home, he was taken out of his thoughts when the vehicle came to a halt. "We've arrived, sir." The new place was located in an older quiet part of Houston's suburbs. As the old man pulled his luggage up the doorsteps, neighbors were peeping out their windows, wondering why a stranger had come. A couple passed by and Xuan bowed. Outside in front, he noticed the paint was peeling off. He opened the door and immediately took his belongings upstairs to the bedroom. Before going upstairs, he took out the folder with his mission's details and set it on the dining room table. Not minding the mess in the house, he sat down and opened it.

For Xuan, every day for the last five years since October 22nd, 1975 was a living hell. Inside the folder, were the profiles of seven American soldiers; seven decorated men who would pay dearly for the crime they had committed.

There were tough immigration screenings in order to come to the United States and many questions Xuan couldn't answer but somehow he made it through. With six months left, Xuan came to do what he only lived for. His good memories of his wife and daughter were fading away as the days passed by. Now that he's seventy years old, a combination of age and time were rapidly taking its toll. The old man knew he had to do something before it was too late.

———

His easiest target would be Tim Marshall; a fucking slob who was old and weak. Xuan had been trailing him and the other six through a Vietnamese friend in the US military for the last two years. He discovered that Tim was a regular at the local hospital in town but didn't know why.

"Bastard!" yelled Xuan as he stared at Tim's photo. Listed in his file were Tim's work address and social security number. By tracking his social, he'd get more information but that was a long shot. For now, Tim's workplace would do and it wouldn't be easy killing him inside there.

The next man was Ben Rogers; a wealthy Texan who owned land up and down the United States and had done quite well for himself financially after the War. Ben had three children and his second wife was half his age. He was spotted often playing at the most prestigious golf clubs around the country. Xuan wondered how he got so rich; growing up in a home with Jewish parents in the ghettos of Houston before he enlisted in the service.

Matthew Jones, the third man; a heavy gambler that lost his home and was now renting a one-bedroom apartment with his wife of twenty years. Matthew has weekly visits scheduled to see a psychiatrist, due to post-traumatic stress disorder.

Xuan then took a sip of tea, setting the three men's files aside and moving onto the next.

Zachary Hamilton served after Vietnam as the right hand of Major General Harris of the Texas Brigade and was well respected amongst the townsmen and military.

As Xuan read further, his heart raced and decided to not to touch the remaining files for the rest of the day. He was ready to go on with his mission to find Tim and longed for the moment to begin tasting redemption.

Someone knocked on the door. Xuan carefully walked slowly towards it, peeking through the hole. A woman in her late forties was there smiling. "Who the fuck is this?" thought Xuan puzzled by this woman's smile. Yet, he opened.

"Hi, I saw you just moved here!"

"Yes, about an hour ago."

"Well, I wanted to welcome you to our little community." The woman then handed Xuan a box. Maybe its a bomb! A thought that crossed Xuan's mind because of its warmth.

"It's right out of the oven."

Xuan wasn't sure what to say. He was never given a welcoming gift from anyone back home.

"Thank you," said Xuan setting the box down on a stand near the door.

"I'm Katherine by the way. Nice to meet you." She offered her hand to shake.

"Xuan Lang." He said shaking hers.

"I'll see you around, and if you need anything, we're always a doorbell away."

She waved goodbye and left. Xuan smiled while shutting the door and returned to his seat, wondering what if someone else will come. The details surrounding the remaining men were vague and Xuan didn't even bother glancing further. He knew he'd catch each one of them sooner or later.

For the remainder of the afternoon, Xuan sipped on a few cups of green tea, reclining in a Lazyboy that the previous owners had left behind and watching the local news until nightfall came.

* * *

Two weeks passed and it was the night of Tim Marshall's birthday. Xuan devised a plan to slip in Tim's party as a waiter. Xuan purchased a black suit and a red tie for the occasion. The old man's slicked hair was too shiny from the mousse. In Texas, he noticed everyone wore cowboy hats but Xuan had forgotten to buy one.

Once the taxi arrived, Xuan got in and the driver asked during the ride, "Are you new here in town?", staring through the rear-view mirror.

"I just arrived this morning."

"Well, Houston's a lovely place. I'm sure you will grow fond of it."

"I hope so," said Xuan staring out the window, realizing that they were downtown from the towering lights of the buildings.

"We're here, sir."

"Thank you and keep the change."

"Thanks, sir. God bless."

Tim's party was held at a high-end restaurant called the Taste of Texas and it was already packed. Xuan made his way through the side exit to the kitchen. A few waiters looked at Xuan but continued working as he strolled past the chef's grill to the lobby.

Tim and his wife arrived a few minutes later, holding each other's hands. The guests made space for the couple and clapped for them as they came inside. Tim looked much older than the picture Xuan had in his file while his wife looked more like his daughter. Tim and his wife walked by Xuan and waved, thanking the guests for coming. Xuan looked for an empty seat at one of the tables and saw one with a group of couples seated. Just as Xuan was about to sit down, a man said, "Excuse me. This seat's already taken, bud."

"Just as I was about to introduce myself. I'm Xuan Lang." The couples looked at him, expecting him to leave.

"Never heard that name before."

A woman among them said, "Be nice fellas. He's obviously new to this town."

"So, are you here for the auction, Xuan or the birthday party?" asked a man opposite of Xuan.

"Auction or Birthday party? That's funny. I guess this is a gathering for the rich and famous." The table laughed at Xuan's response.

"What business do you have here in Texas, Xuan?" asked another man at the far end of the table.

"Herbs! I own an herb shop." This was partly true. Back in Vietnam, Xuan opened one, but was forced to close down when his family was killed. *This business might make money here. What an excellent idea!*

"And is this business of yours profitable?" a man asked as the others at the table laughed wildly.

"Why would I keep doing it if it wasn't?"

The man frowned at Xuan's sarcasm. "I see. Maybe we can talk about it more over dinner."

———

An hour passed and the hall's lights began dimming. Tim and his wife walked to the podium in the middle of the room.

"Finally, it's starting," a woman said clasping her hands. She was a close friend of Tim.

Xuan's eyes were fixed on Tim; studying his every movement and largely ignoring the claps from the audience.

"Ladies, Gentleman." Tim grabbed the microphone as he waved. "I'm thrilled you all could join us tonight."

As Xuan listened, a group of men brought out some expensive paintings, one by one and some other valuables.

"We'll now begin," announced Tim's wife, smiling uncontrollably.

The crowd then became silent, waiting. Xuan had enough money to participate and thought it might be a way to start a friendship with Tim in order to get closer to the others.

"First up is the Marionette Vase from the 19th

century," proclaimed Tim pointing. Xuan kept quiet as it wasn't something he didn't see value in.

"Eight hundred dollars!" Tim's wife's words echoed through the hall.

"Nine!" a woman yelled behind Xuan as her husband disapproved.

"Nine hundred dollars." Tim pointed at the woman.

"One thousand!" a voice from another table yelled.

"One thousand and two hundred!" another man quickly followed up.

"Pathetic. So much for an object with such little importance!" A thought that crossed Xuan's mind as the bidding was taking place.

"Sold!" A woman in red hair cheered, clapping loudly.

Next up was a painting, which resembled something that Xuan's wife would have made. It brought back memories of the happier moments in his life and he couldn't let this reminder slip away.

"Starting at five hundred dollars."

"Six hundred!" one man yelled a few feet away from him.

"Seven hundred!" Xuan raised his hand.

Everybody turned their attention to the old Asian man; a new face in town.

The attention soon faded when another person bidded higher. "Nine hundred."

Xuan didn't think that this painting would be worth this much, but he continued. "One thousand."

No one else was willing to bid higher. Content with his possession, Xuan poured himself a glass of wine.

"Sold!" Tim announced.

Xuan raised his glass in thanks.

The auction continued on for another hour, and Xuan started conversing with the men and women at the table. Sadly, Xuan couldn't get close to Tim, even though he had his eyes on him for most of the evening.

"All the owners of tonight's auction who spent over $1,000, please come this way," announced Tim's wife.

Xuan got up and followed the others through a back door. He along with four others entered and waited until Tim's wife had arrived.

"Congratulations, ladies and gentlemen." The young woman introduced herself as Anna standing in front of the valuables.

She then ordered for the men to bring drinks.

Anna noticed Xuan sitting by himself and walked over, "Excuse me, sir. You've chosen one of my dearest pieces."

Xuan almost choked wiping his mouth. His expression made her laugh. He set his glass down and said, "I'll be sure to cherish it."

"My husband forced me to sell it. We've been having financial problems lately." Anna paused. "Stupid me! I've shouldn't had said that."

"It's fine. We're all human and have financial problems sometimes in life." "Well, now I'm sure my little secret is safe with you."

"You have my word," smiled Xuan.

Tim's got financial problems, huh? Xuan thought as he pictured how he would use that weakness against him as Anna kept talking. Then their conversation was cut short by Tim who grabbed Anna by the waist and pulled her towards him.

"You must be the infamous Xuan Lang."

"That's right except for the infamous part."

"My wife and I would like to invite you to dinner tomorrow night. All winners are invited. It would be a shame if you didn't show up." Tim was looking more at his wife than Xuan.

"I'll think about it, but thank you for the offer."

"Please, do. You'll meet some great men and women in this town."

Tim didn't like men near his wife. She was young and busty and at times, flirtatious. Xuan got up and walked around, small-talking with the other bidders in the room. He knew he'd left a bad first impression with Tim who'd probably was thinking he was flirting with Anna.

CHAPTER TWO

Xuan was nowhere near being ready. His room was covered with clothes; feeling he didn't pack enough and decided to wear the suit he wore at the funeral of his family.

It reminded him of the mission that he had set out for. Five years ago, his wife was raped by the Americans officers; one being Vietnamese. They then murdered his daughter in cold blood lighting the house on fire. Xuan was out at work and came home heartbroken; seeing the men savagely destroy his life before his very eyes.

The Vietnam War left unbearable scars. Putting on this suit was one of many scars that Xuan Lang would always remember. The last time he wore it, he was reminded of his angels going to the heavens.

Sighing, he buttoned it up and straightened his posture in front of the mirror. Tonight, Xuan knew he'd have to look presentable.

A taxi came by to take him to Tim's home. As they rode through the streets, Xuan thought about him not saying a word to his neighbors. It's been almost ten days since he arrived and he knew that they were watching him. They had to, simply for the fact that he was the only Asian in the neighborhood of military veteran families. Since there was heavy traffic, he knew he'd be at least fifteen minutes late. Tim and Anna didn't seem to mind and welcomed him telling him to come right in.

"We've been expecting you, Xuan." Anna embraced him as Tim looked on, jealous.

"Traffic was a nightmare! I'm sorry."

The house was a mansion, and it was strange that a person who had financial problems could afford living here.

There was jazz playing in the background and Xuan heard laughter. Xuan's breathing hitched when he spotted four men; all who were responsible for the death of his family. They were seated at a wooden table, laughing.

"Where are the other three?" thought Xuan referring to Joshua Warren, Ronald Ravens, and Duong

Gian. Duong was an interpreter contracted by the US Marines and was the main culprit leading the rape of Xuan's wife as Xuan and his daughter watched.

"Please take a seat," said Anna breaking Xuan's thoughts. The feeling of seeing these men sent chills through the old man's body. He wanted to lunge and stab them to death but he had to remain calm and patient.

He sat in silence, listening to a few men who showed up for the special gathering but the bidders hadn't arrived yet. After a few refreshments and chatting with the guests, Tim and Anna finally joined everyone at the table, clicking their wine glasses to get everyone's attention. "Unfortunately, the buyers from last night's auction will not be able to join us today except for Mr. Xuan Lang. Fellas be nice as we'd like to say cheers for new friendships."

The men stopped talking and stood up.

"Cheers to that," a man by the name of Zachary spoke as the group laughed.

"Now, I hope our food appeases your taste buds. Anna tried her best here," said Tim as he hugged Anna.

Xuan didn't see Anna as serious. She was young and looked as if she was always out of the home perhaps with her girlfriends more than Tim.

"It smells delicious," said Ben staring at the food.

"Please, dig in gentleman," said Anna.

Xuan took a few slices of roast beef, mashed potatoes, and salad. When he took a bite, he was ready to spit it out. Anna's cooking was nowhere near complimentary. She should have hired a catering service instead. As Xuan ate, he had the urge to vomit, shutting his eyes to avoid its dullness.

"How do you like the food, Xuan?"

Tim looked at Xuan strangely as even he was having second thoughts about his wife's cooking.

"One of the best meals I've had in a while."

"I'm so flattered, you've just made my day, Xuan," giggled Anna as Tim watched her reaction.

Tim was a dick. After a few words with Anna, he cleared his throat. "Gentlemen, you haven't told me about what you've been working on lately." He turned his focus on the three cowards opposite to Xuan.

"Don't act as if you don't know, Tim. We've been struggling as of late with the new city ordinances, but I think we'll be open for business soon," said Matthew as he wiped his mouth with a cloth.

"What kind of company are you gentlemen springing up, if you don't mind me asking?" The men turned their attention to the old man as Anna stuffed herself, not wanting to be a part of the conversation.

"A new car dealership," said Zachary.

"That's smart. Do you think it could make big money out here?"

"Why wouldn't it? The roads are being improved daily and many are looking to buying new cars before a recession hits. Damn, Reagan is coming in office in a few months," said Matthew.

"I must admit there's still a lot of work to be done," added Zachary.

Xuan wasn't interested in anything they had to say but wanted to build a relationship to get closer to the men. As they chatted on, all of them had a different outlook on the business.

Then Zachary broke the ice, "That's why I have these two buds by my side," grinned Zachary as he hugged Matthew and Duong, pulling them tightly.

Xuan felt defeated by their happiness and wanted to change topics. "Hopefully, I'll find some friends as true as you before I die."

"I truly hope you do, my little Asian friend," answered Matthew sarcastically.

"By the way, I'm Xuan Lang."

"Where are you from?" asked Ben, seemingly curious by Xuan's name.

"I'm from the Philippines."

"What business do you have here in America?" probed Matthew.

"I'm opening an herb shop not too far from downtown." Xuan expected them to laugh.

"That's an unusual career for a man your age," said Matthew. The men were maybe ten years younger, so it was funny how they looked down on the old man. *"Fucking Americans."* Xuan took another bite of the bland roast beef.

"It truly is but an old man has a passion for fixing people."

"Don't we all?" exclaimed Tim raising his glass as everyone followed.

———

Within an hour and a half, Xuan wrapped up the paperwork and took possession of his painting. Just as he was about to leave, Zachary came over to him, "Xuan, we'd be honored if you could spare us some of your time this week and go golfing with us."

"Why are you inviting me? You don't even know why I'm here." Xuan was thinking as Zachary spoke.

"We feel bad for treating you the way we did in the beginning. Our little town is not used to strangers. Since most of us come from military families, we have a code of honor. Please accept our apologies."

"Ok, I'll accept that and think about it."

* * *

The next morning, Xuan was awakened by loud knocks. Xuan came downstairs in his pajamas and opened the door. Standing there, was his neighbor Katherine.

"Xuan, I didn't mean to wake you," Katherine said looking at Xuan puzzled.

"Oh no, Katherine, it's fine. How can I help you?" Xuan grabbed the handle of the door, resting on it.

"The owners couldn't get a hold of you yesterday," said Katherine taking out a folder.

"I've been pretty busy these days. Sorry!"

"Well, they said the house comes in a package deal with the store they own."

"A store? Why didn't they mention this before?" Xuan opened the door, inviting her inside. There were boxes of empty Chinese food on the table. "Sorry for the mess, I haven't had guests yet." He set a case to the side and directed her to the sofa.

"It's fine." Katherine opened the folder, taking out

the papers. "The owners had a convenience store, but it failed miserably. Let's say they weren't keeping stock like they were supposed to."

Xuan wondered what happened as it looked like Katherine wasn't fond of them.

"Is the store nearby?"

"Yes, just down on the corner, but I have to admit that it needs some fixing." Katherine chuckled as she handed Xuan the folder. "You'll need to sign here and I'll mail it to them. They are away on vacation in Maui for God knows how long." After reading over everything, Xuan signed off and handed the contract back. As Katherine was leaving, she left the remaining papers and keys to the store on the table.

———

Xuan retired close to five years ago from the army and opened his first business in selling herbs after the tragedy. He was given his pension and lived a simple life. However, fate played with him dearly. Countless times, he blamed God for his unfortunate happenings. He was a man destroyed by those who destroyed his family.

As Katherine closed the door, Xuan was anxious to know of the store's condition. He changed quickly and headed down the road, remembering Katherine's directions vaguely. As he walked, he almost started doubting her. "Maybe I'm on the wrong road?" After passing by a few stores, he saw some bold letters written on the front of a closed storefront reading - "Seamans." Xuan fumbled the keys while unlocking the door, excited about going inside.

He looked around, seeing the store was full of dust and cobwebs. "A free store but a lot of work," questioned the old man if this shop had a chance of turning a profit.

Xuan graduated from college in holistic medicine and knew almost every herb that existed. Slowly, a vision of how to set up the place was already being planted. What about the customers. Do they use holistic remedies? The location seemed perfect, and by it not having any pharmacies close by, the business could flourish.

There were boxes stacked up to the ceiling in the back storage room, almost tumbling over when Xuan opened the door. The area was smaller than the front but big enough to stock inventory. The paint on the wall was peeling off, but there were a sink and other appliances. Not being able to tolerate the mess any longer, Xuan started putting the boxes on top of one another and pushing them aside to one corner.

"Xuan!?"

Katherine's voice startled him, making him jump. She was holding plastic bags and from Xuan's conclusion, she'd just done grocery shopping.

"You scared me." He said, dusting off his hands.

"Sorry, I was passing by from the market and saw the door open. I didn't think you were coming here right away."

"Yeah, I wanted to give the place a good look. I have time today." Xuan sat down on an old chair in the center of the room.

"I'm impressed. I thought you would leave it be and didn't want anything to do with it. For sure, you proved me wrong."

"How could I not?" Xuan stood up and walked Katherine to the front area, where an old cash register was left behind. "This could be put to use. If we can put a little muscle in this old shop, it would be nice," hinted Xuan

"You're right. It's an excellent idea opening an herbal shop yourself in this neighborhood. There are always sick people here. Many got ill when returning from the War," said Katherine following behind Xuan and looking around.

"I'm planning for just that. By the way, do they have this time of shop around here?"

"Oh my, no!" Katherine said, setting aside her bags. "And I'd be glad to spread the word about the business for you. I know everyone in this area."

"So, this sounds like a partnership?" laughed Xuan.

"I guess so. Where should I start?" She rolled up her sleeves, placing her hands on her hips, ready.

"There is a lot of dirt," said Xuan pointing to the floor. "We can start here. Let me pay for some supplies."

"No, no. I have enough at home." Katherine went home and brought the supplies back and Xuan realized it would be a longer day than usual.

Xuan began cleaning what he could until Katherine returned. The plumbing wasn't working properly in the back as the sink clogged. After many attempts to unclog it, Xuan sighed, "This is useless," sitting down on one of the stools and wiping his forehead. The shop's bell chimed and Katherine walked in, donning a pair of gloves, fully ready.

"Isn't this a bit over the top?" asked Xuan.

"Not at all, have you seen this place?" She set a bucket down, placing her hands on her hips while looking around.

"It's not as bad as you think it is. You'll see, partner." She started by dumping the boxes, one by one outside. Then, she went to the storage shelves, clearing out the outdated cans of food and other rubbish. Xuan had the easiest chore, sweeping the rooms and putting trash from Katherine in the dumpster.

After four hours, they finished and Xuan was tired even though he didn't work as hard. He invited Katherine over for coffee which she did after bathing. She told Xuan she was a nurse at the local hospital and had two children in college. Her new husband's a bank accountant who's barely home and always away. Xuan then told her about his family back in Vietnam. Before midnight, Katherine had left. Xuan saw Katherine as a nice person to have as a partner but knew not to trust her with his mission. Then, he sat regretting about allowing her to get close to him. The old man vowed not to let anyone inside.

———

Xuan didn't know whether to accept Tim's invitation to go golfing or not. Inside, he came up with many excuses. He never wanted to see their faces again, but he must. Xuan was confused, realizing that he had no gear for the occasion. The only thing that resembled golf in his possession was a green polo shirt. When his phone rang in the wee hours of the morning, it caught the old man off-guard. He stumbled down the staircase to hurry and answer it.

"Hello?"

"Xuan?"

"Who's this?" Xuan knew who it was.

"Zachary." How the hell did he get my number?

"I'm calling to make sure if you're coming tonight at six, pal?"

Xuan cleared his throat after a long silence. "Yeah, sure. Why at six? Isn't it late?"

"Bud, golf is fun at night. Believe me, you'll see."

"If you say so."

"All right, I'll see you at the Walden. Don't forget —" added Zachary.

Before he hung up, Xuan asked, "Wait, how did you get my number?"

"I got it from Tim. He has your information from the auction, remember?"

Xuan never thought Tim would give his contact information. "I see. Thanks, see you later, Zach." Xuan ran back upstairs to his closet, raging inside. Furthermore, he didn't have a precise plan on how he was going to kill all seven. He put on his shirt and would leave everything else to the guys.

The 6 o'clock hour came quickly and the weather

outside was warm and mild. Xuan didn't have any emotion about meeting his least favored individuals. Now, it feels like he's sleeping with the enemy.

The Walden Golf Club was only a few miles away. By the looks of the outside, it was sealed off from the public. Xuan fastened his duffle bag over his shoulder and walked inside. The reception was high-end and the ceiling had pictures engraved of some of the world's most famous golfers. The staff greeted everyone warmly and the old man didn't have a clue where he was headed. How would Zachary know I arrived? He stood close by the receptionist desk, patiently waiting.

For close to fifteen minutes, many passed by, all wearing polo shirts and white shorts. They matched the people he saw on an American show called "The Loveboat," but its subtitles were in Vietnamese. As the old man started drifting away in thought, a voice startled him.

"Xuan!"

"Xuan!"

Xuan turned, seeing seven men coming to the reception area; Joshua, Ronald, Ben, Matthew, Tim, Zachary, and Duong Gian.

He was taken aback by their presence, tumbling back as the striking memory of his family's murder resurfaced. Those men have no shame and didn't know Xuan was here to settle the score once and for all. No one knew what these cowards had done, and Xuan Lang was planning on exposing all.

"Good day, gentlemen." Xuan held out his hand to shake theirs.

"Are you ready?" chuckled Zachary.

The others laughed, probably because of Xuan's outfit. They were dressed in white pants and blue polo shirts. A few of them were wearing USA caps and it was hilarious. "You all may be dressed like Arnold Palmer, but I have what it takes to beat you." The joke was corny, but the men grinned.

"Nice one, Xuan," said Matthew, grabbing him on the shoulder. "My new Asian friend, Xuan Lang. You've met Tim of course, Ben and Zachary."

As Matthew introduced him to the others, Xuan looked at them straight in the eye. There was no backing down now. This was a dangerous game, and the seven criminals were the players.

"Joshua Warren." The man had blonde hair and bright blue eyes. By his looks, he seemed unfriendly as if he was having a bad day.

Xuan continued to the second one on his left.

"I'm Ronald Ravens." Ronald took both Xuan's

hands trying to mimic an Asian salute of some sort. He had a wrinkled face and seemed kind.

Xuan had second thoughts on turning to the last. "Duong Gian. I think we met a few days ago. You're from the Philippines, right?"

"Oh, oh yes! We sure did," stuttered Xuan.

Right away, Xuan recognized Duoug's accent.

"This way," Tim stated, walking to the sliding doors of the patio. Tim and Ben carried the golf balls while the caddies took the clubs and rest of the equipment. Ronald held the keys to the golf carts. The group of men followed behind and saw the golf course light up from a distance, contrasting the dusk.

Xuan stared in awe at the beautiful view while the others had seen it many times before. After walking down a long set of stairs to the area of the golf carts, Xuan jumped inside with Joshua, Zachary, and Tim. The others paired up and drove ahead.

The endless terrain of the green was reeling leaving Xuan in a trance. The warmness of the evening sun was getting the better of him. It started becoming hotter than the daylight and Xuan knew it was his blood boiling. As they neared their portion of the course, Xuan started imagining where these guys learned how to play.

"Do you know how to golf, Xuan?" yelled Tim from the front seat.

"Honestly, I do not, but I'll learn from you, guys tonight."

"So, you won't beat us after all. Bud, It's easy. All you have to do is put the ball in the hole." Tim and Zachary chuckled at Joshua's description.

"It's settled then; I'm good at that."

The men roared like wild animals and Xuan wasn't impressed.

The cart came to a sudden screech, and everyone jumped out. "Finally, we get to have a rematch," shouted Ben from the other side. Then they gathered in a circle to divide the teams into fours while the caddies prepared the course.

"I think we should split up like before since we already know who's with whom. We'll take Xuan," uttered Matthew.

Xuan believed they would surely lose now. He wasn't good at sports.

"I see you're lucky." Duong came beside Xuan.

"Let the best team win, fellas," yelled Ben.

"You're first dickheads," taunted Tim. Xuan was grouped with Matthew, Tim, and Joshua while Ronald, Duong, Ben, and Zachary were the challengers.

Eighteen holes of golf will make it a long evening. Ronald had hired some college-women caddies to spark up things. Ben was the first one to start. Setting the golf ball on the tee and gripping the club tightly, he focused on his swing while sweating profusely.

Ben hit the ball and it landed near to the hole, almost going in. The caddies clapped and kissed Ben as his teammates cheered him on.

"I see you got better than the last time," mocked Joshua.

They continued, taking turns until it was Xuan's. His team gave him instructions while the opposing team mimicked the way he clutched the golf club. Xuan calculated the distance from the ball to the hole almost resembling a professional. When he swung, the golf ball flew across a little left of his target but close enough for a bogey.

His teammates clapped, surprised at the old man. Zachary whistled, taunting Xuan. "So many fake people," thought Xuan. Now, it was time to focus on getting the ball inside the hole. Xuan walked to the spot with the caddies, measuring the distance mentally as he approached. He then swung, resulting the ball going inside the hole. Everyone cheered and one of the caddies hugged Xuan while kissing him on the cheek. The guys laughed, seeing Xuan uneasiness.

"Cheer up, bud. The girl likes you," said Matthew.

"Not my cup of tea."

"Haha."

Now, it was Tim's turn. Xuan didn't pay much attention, tuning into Duong and Joshua's conversation. Xuan walked over to join in.

"I already started the shipment and it will reach Vietnam in about two to three days, tops." Duong lowered his voice as he saw Xuan approaching. They cleared their throats when he walked up.

"Gentlemen. I'm impressed. An amazing job for an old hag, am I right?" joked Xuan about himself, causing them to laugh. While the others played, the three began chatting.

"Don't joke around like that, Xuan. We are honorable military men. There is no pride. This is a friendly game of golf. We've allowed you in our little circle. Be a little bit more humble." Duong saw the seriousness of Joshua while Xuan was clearly puzzled.

"Hey man, I'm kidding." All three burst in laughter.

"You know I was about to kill you," returned Xuan giggling.

"I bet you were," joked Joshua.

"Duong!" Ben called. "It's your turn, you fucking cunt."

The men and the caddies started moving to the next hole and Duong was excited to show what he could do. He put on a show, striking the ball right in the hole without hesitation. Surely, Duong played this game many times before as it appeared he was the best player in the group.

Everyone clapped, and within the next two hours, they were at the last hole. Tired and sweaty, the sun had already started set. The match was thrilling, but for Xuan, he couldn't wait to go.

Tim was the last to go, and to the team's dismay, it ended it with a total error, leaving Duong's team to win. Xuan's first target, Tim was sad and the old man put his arm around him to comfort him.

———

After the match, Tim invited Xuan for a drink at his house and as much as he didn't want to go, he came along.

When they pulled up to Tim's, Tim noticed his living room's lights were dimmed and Anna's car was parked in the garage. "Lord, this woman will want to talk all night," thought Tim. They rang the doorbell and waited for his wife to answer. "Why doesn't he have the key? Strange!" thought Xuan. She didn't answer but there was some bustle coming from behind the door. Someone was inside. Tim banged on the door nonstop.

"Anna! Open up right now or I'll fucking kill you!" When she didn't, Tim kicked the door down and stared.

His wife was half naked while a young man was climbing out of the kitchen window, naked with his clothes in his hands. She froze at the sight of Tim and Xuan. Tim ran to the kitchen, pushing Anna down to the ground and out of the way to catch the guy, but he was gone.

"What the fuck have you done?"

"Tim, please I can explain." Anna picked up the leftover pieces of clothing off the couch. Xuan watched, started.

"You have nothing to explain. Save yourself the humiliation. How could the fuck could you do this to me?" Tim's voice was cracked and he was about to cry. Xuan couldn't believe this was playing out like a movie.

"He is just a co-worker. We were—"

"I don't care who he is. This is my house, and you

don't get to disrespect me like this." He pointed around. "Get your stuff and get the fuck out now! I'll be having my lawyer write up the divorce papers in the morning."

Tim sat on the couch; the same one Anna had been making out on. Xuan remained standing, not knowing what to do or say. Xuan partly smiled, knowing Tim had it coming.

Anna came down the stairs, with her mascara smeared down her eyes from her crying. "I love you, Tim." Those were her last words.

The scene worsened when Tim started weeping. Xuan had no choice but to comfort him. "Kill him now! Frame Anna" imagined Xuan.

"Listen, it will get better." Tim didn't respond, resting his head on his hands, breathing out wearily.

"It won't, Xuan. She's the only woman I love more than my own life."

"Women like her don't deserve your love, Tim. I'm sure you'll find someone worthy." The night's winds rushed inside from door being left open and Xuan got up to shut it.

The night passed as Tim kept crying over Anna while Xuan patiently listened. Xuan excused himself to use the restroom. He sneaked into Tim's bedroom, opened his drawers, spotting papers of bank transfers and receipts to Anna. Tim had spent a fortune on jewelry, rental cars, and hair appointments for her. Xuan remembered Anna talking about their money problems and she was responsible for them.

Xuan came back downstairs, finding Tim in the same spot. His vulnerability was to Xuan's advantage and killing him would be easier than the old man thought.

"Tim, I'm sorry bud, but I have to go. I have work in the morning." Tim escorted Xuan to the door and didn't say a single word.

"Take it easy, Bud. I'll check on you tomorrow."

Xuan finished planning for his first kill - Tim Marshall. It would be harder than expected since Tim was working long hours trying to forget about Anna. Two weeks had passed since Xuan had last seen Tim. Tim called Xuan yesterday, inviting him to hang out after work, and told him to meet him at his job at five. Xuan told Tim if he wasn't there by 5, he'd have to reschedule due to a large shipment of herbs coming in.

Earlier in the week, Xuan got his firearm license in the mail. The old man had no problems getting one now that he's running a business. Texas' gun laws were so lax he only had to show a copy of the renter's contract for the store. Xuan needed only one gun to finish off what he came to America for.

Xuan studied the revolver, a Baretta 92F, lying on the table. He was ready and as he put on his coat, the doorbell sounded. It was Katherine. Xuan placed the gun in his coat pocket and proceed to the door.

"Xuan, sorry to bother you. May I ask a favor?"

"Yes, sure."

"My youngest is over for the weekend, and his temperature isn't going down."

"Give me a minute and I'll be right out."

"Ok."

Xuan closed the door, took out the gun and it, then placed it in a flowerpot nearby and came outside. Katherine hurried as Xuan had never seen her like this before. They reached her home and proceeded to her son's room at the far end of the hallway. He was laying in bed, scarcely breathing and sweating heavily.

"I gave him medicine this morning, but his temperature isn't dropping. From what I see, he has a high fever." Katherine gave Xuan a plastic chair and the old man looked over the young man. The scene reminded Xuan of his wife, Binh whenever she was sick. The old man deeply reflected as he closely monitored Katherine's son.

"I have some herbs that may help." Katherine handed Xuan a plastic bag in which he saw White

Willow. That herb was discovered thousands of years ago by Chinese doctors and oddly, Katherine had them.

"You'll need to make him tea with this White Willow." Xuan handed her the herb, and Katherine rushed to the kitchen. After finding Yarrow inside the bag also, he joined Katherine to make another treatment. Xuan took elderflower, peppermint, boneset, cayenne, and ginger from Katherines's counter and told her it would be the perfect blend. Katherine finished making the first blend and rushed back. Xuan came inside minutes later, giving the young man his medicine and watched his response as the young man's sweat began to decrease. Katherine jumped up in joy, embracing Xuan. Then, Xuan excused himself, as he was a man on a mission.

———

Xuan scouted the area before Tim left from work, discovering an alleyway nearby. It would be the ideal place to execute Tim with nothing but junkies' things left behind. Waiting outside, Xuan watched the workers as they left for the day. His leather jacket didn't stop the fall's wind from entering. As the clock reached 5:10, Xuan wondered if Tim was bullshitting him. The old man arrived over two hours ago, so another a few minutes wouldn't hurt.

A little boy came up to Xuan, selling a newspaper, and he kindly declined. "I'm sorry." Subsequently, Tim came to the front entrance, looking disturbed. His hair was rumpled, and his shirt was half-open. His troubled expression stood out as he walked slowly, often looking behind as if he was expecting something bad to happen. Xuan was waiting far enough that Tim couldn't spot him. It was 5:32 and Xuan already gave him a heads-up about not coming. The only thing Xuan wanted was for Tim to walk through that alley. The pistol felt cold against the old man's skin. It would be his first murder, and he felt high-strung.

Tim turned down another block, catching Xuan off-guard, as the old man almost collided into a pole. The sound caught Tim's attention, and Xuan quickly hid behind a dumpster. The moment was getting close as Tim getting closer to that alleyway. Xuan checked the surroundings and there was no one in sight. The streets were almost empty, making an escape fairly easy. He then ran up to Tim from behind. The old man pulled out the Baretta and aimed; the cold barrel pressed up against the back of Tim's head made him stop. Tim placed his hands in the air thinking someone was robbing him. Xuan smiled speculating about this bastard's final seconds.

Tim turned around and his eyes widened. "What are you doing, Xuan?" Xuan didn't immediately answer. Two worlds collided in the strangest of manners and yet it will be ashes to ashes, dust to dust for one.

"It's time to pay for what you've done." Xuan's voice shivered violently, ignoring Tim's endless sobs. Tim pleaded to Xuan why was he doing this.

"My wife, my daughter." Xuan pulled out two photos, holding them up. Tim was at a loss of words. He remembered and felt ashamed. Tim's weeping only grew louder.

"What do you have to say, you fucking bastard before I kill you?" yelled Xuan regretting he hadn't already done so.

"I'm sorry, please don't." Tim dropped to his knees, crying. "We were drunk fucks. Ok? It wasn't my fault." Xuan stood there shaking his head in disbelief.

"Well, this is mine." Xuan shot Tim in the head. His body slammed on the cold ground and the old man stared, relishing the display of blood pouring. He knew Houston's news stations would be flooded with the death of their decorated marine, Tim

Marshall. Xuan promised himself the other executions would be more extreme.

———

Two days had passed since Tim Marshall's death and Xuan was walking through the Galleria looking for a gift for Katherine's son. He thought about buying a watch but had trouble finding a good one.

The Galleria was packed, and Xuan had already been to his third watch store. On the top floor, he spotted a decent jewelry store. A gentleman was wrapping up with a customer when an old lady came from behind the counter. "Hi, how can I help you today?" "Can you show me your best watch? I've looked around and haven't seen anything good yet."

"Sir. why of course." The lady smiled and went behind the counter, pulling out a black box. "This is my favorite. I'm sure it will tickle your fancy." She brought a Gold Seiko with a slick black leather band. Xuan looked at it for a long time, knowing the young man would like it. He wasn't easily defeated by an illness like his daughter.

The woman gift-wrapped the watch and the old man felt happy for once. He even strolled around the mall for a few hours before heading to Katherine's.

She'd invited him over for dinner at seven, and now it was close to six. Xuan wanted to look presentable, so he bought himself an outfit at the mall.

Tim Marshall's funeral was held earlier in the day and Xuan excused himself, offering his deepest condolences. Joshua called Xuan the night before and Xuan acted shocked by Tim's passing. Xuan was arrived back home around 6:30 and after getting dressed, went downstairs to watch the news. The news coverage had a picture of Tim in the military and a quote enveloped in an American banner. The news reporter mentioned police were still searching for his killer and asked for the public's help in doing so. "Why is Tim's death getting so much coverage? He was an auctioneer overpricing his pieces of shit," shouted Xuan.

The news anchor kept sobbing as if she knew Tim personally. "Tim Marshall was Houston's face of auctions for years. We will forever remember his bid calling. It's a shame his life ended so violently." Xuan turned the TV off, not wanting to hear anymore. Whatever they know about Tim, was a lie. The man was wicked, and he deserved it.

———

Xuan left to go to Katherine's house and for the first time, he greeted his neighbors. They were baffled seeing an Asian man in their area.

Xuan rang Katherine's doorbell twice and she opened the door, embracing him in a hug. "Come inside, please." Xuan smelled the food as soon as he walked in. It seemed Katherine cooked better than Anna.

"Make yourself at home. My son Ethan will be down shortly." Katherine touched Xuan and he smiled. "Is she flirting with me?"

"Tell him to hurry. I have something for him," said Xuan holding up a bag.

"You shouldn't have. That boy has everything."

Katherine to go back to the kitchen and Xuan sat in the living room. To him, it was strange how American families were when getting to know them. Unlike the many Americans in Vietnam who were going around looking for prostitutes and drugs. As Xuan meditated, Katherine's son entered, introducing himself.

"Good day sir. I'm Ethan." The young man bowed respectfully surprising Xuan.

"Ethan, I'm Xuan. It's a pleasure to meet you in better spirits." Xuan urged him to sit down beside him. "Are you feeling better?"

Ethan was puzzled this strange man was asking about his condition. Xuan realized Ethan didn't recognize him from the other day.

"You had a fever the other day. Your mother and I helped take it away."

"Oh yes, sir. Thank you for the herbs. I feel much better now."

Xuan reached into his bag and took out the black box. "Call me Xuan." Ethan smiled as the old man handed the box to him.

Before Ethan opened it, Katherine walked in carrying plates of food; roast beef with gravy, mashed potatoes, salad, and corn on the cob.

"Hopefully, you'll enjoy this. It took my whole day and I need a new oven," said Katherine wiping the sweat off her forehead. Xuan valued her time even if the food would taste bad. Judging from the smell, it would be better than Anna's.

"You deserve a cooking award, Mom," laughed Ethan, forgetting to say grace while eating.

Katherine slapped him in back of the head. "The guest goes first and what about grace, dear. You remember?"

Ethan froze staring at Xuan, disappointed. "Yes, mom. I'm sorry."

"Now say grace and let's eat."

Katherine joined them after getting a few cups from the kitchen.

Xuan praised Katherine repeatedly as the three entertained in lengthy conversations, forgetting about their concerns. He learned a lot about Ethan and saw many similarities between the young man and his daughter, Binh. Suddenly, a hope sparked in him to spend time with the young man. Reasonably, as a way to fill the gap in Xuan's heart. He envisioned Binh looking down on him happily.

"So, Xuan," asked Ethan. "Why did you move to Texas?"

"Ethan, I think we should draw the line there and give Xuan privacy," stated Katherine.

Ethan lowered his head. "Sorry again, mom."

"It's okay," Xuan reassured Katherine. "I wanted to open my herb business in America. It will be good for Americans to experience different sorts of healing." Xuan answer was complex but enough for Ethan to comprehend.

"I'm curious about these herbs' ability to treat. Are they better than our medicines?" asked Ethan.

Xuan took a sip. "I wondered that too when I was your age, young man. My mother always had many herbs laying around our kitchen, and I grew interested. Little did I know, I would become an herbal expert later in life."

Ethan and Katherine laughed as the spirit in the house felt calm.

"I wonder, now that summer is almost here. Would you have a job opening at your store?" asked Ethan. Clearly, it was the last thing Xuan expected to hear. Many teens focused on school in Vietnam until graduation and did little odd jobs if they weren't.

"Ethan," warned Katherine, playing with her food. She was afraid her son was annoying Xuan.

"I've been looking for someone since your mom did all the work with fixing everything and we're now partners. I think your hands could do me some good." Xuan gave him a handshake agreement and Ethan accepted.

"Thank you, Xuan. It's such an honor." Then, Katherine warned Ethan if he didn't listen to Xuan, she'd send him back home to his father for the summer. After supper, they played cards and Xuan lost every match. Ethan was winning and Katherine accused him of cheating. It was fun ever for Xuan.

"I have to excuse myself. I'm feeling a bit tired."

"Ok, Xuan. Thanks for coming." Katherine and Ethan then walked Xuan to the door.

"Oh! Before I forget. Ethan, come on Saturday for your first day of work."

———

It was Ethan's first day, and he was more excited he was out of college than starting work. The young man was top of his class, and Xuan respected that. Ethan might have had a girlfriend but didn't reveal much.

"Where should I place this, Xuan?" he asked while unpacking a big box filled with commodities.

"Line them up on the shelves. It'll look like we have many things for sale. Don't you agree?"

"I do."

While Ethan was stacking the items, in came Xuan's first customer; a middle-aged man, who seemed worried. "Do you need help with anything, sir?"

"Do you have any rosemary and chamomile?" The man went in his pockets, taking out a few coins. Xuan knew he was poor and it saddened him. "Sure, sir."

Ethan helped, and the man asked the price, counting his coins.

"Your total is two dollars but—" paused Xuan as the man went to give him the money.

"It's on me."

Ethan packed the herbs and gave them to the man who smiled thanking them.

After the man left, Ethan had nothing but praises for Xuan. "We must help when we have it," remarked Xuan.

Xuan went to the back and picked out one of the newspapers from the heap of mail at the door. Reading the front-page, it took him by surprise when he saw Tim's widow's interview mentioned on Page 3. She talked about Tim, telling that their marriage was the best time of her life and how she couldn't imagine living without him. "Such lies," Xuan deemed. The old man shook his head and turned the page.

The day went by quickly with Xuan was tallying up the inventory in the back. Ethan didn't bother Xuan as he was needed out front. When Xuan and Ethan were ready to leave for the evening, a man was waiting outside the door, startling Ethan.

"Zachary!?"

"I was the man but not no more. Oh God! Tim's gone." His words slurred as it appeared Tim had been drinking.

Xuan told Ethan to go, telling him the guy was a companion. "Ok, Xuan. See you tomorrow." Xuan tucked the shop's keys in his pocket while he walked over to Zachary. "What the hell are you doing here?" asked Xuan. Zachary stumbled with his face landing in Xuan's chest. Xuan pushed him away but It was clear Zachary was too drunk to walk. A car rode by seeing Zachary and the driver shouted his name but he didn't stop.

Xuan had no plans of killing him yet. He could have just left him on the sidewalk but Xuan carried Zachary to his house. He laid Zach down on his couch, hearing his heavy breathing that rocked the living room. The smell of alcohol scented the entire downstairs.

"Tim's gone and now others are alone." Zachary's words caught Xuan's attention as he took his shoes off, kicking them aside.

"What do you mean?"

"They think someone is after them after all these years. It's probably because it's—" Zachary's words stopped. He dozed off asleep. The only thing stopping the old man was Ethan who saw Zach and could implicate Xuan being the last person to be with him. Xuan went through Zachary's belongings and found only curled up dollars. He let Zach sleep in peace; a word that shouldn't be associated with this monster. Xuan went upstairs and knew he would gather more in the morning when Zachary was sober.

———

It was morning and Xuan Lang couldn't sleep well because of Zachary who was still asleep. Xuan went downstairs to wake him; stomping loud on the wooden steps. Xuan sensed Zach's loud snoring disturbed his neighbors. The old man cleared his throat at the bottom of the stairs, waking Zachary who jumped up in fear.

"Morning, Zach." Zachary rubbed his eyes while coughing.

"Xuan." Zachary hesitated, straightening himself up. Xuan came for one reason; a confession resulting from last night.

"I must've crashed here. Huh?" said Zachary tripping over his shoes.

"You did and coming to my shop drunk wasn't a good sign of faith. You scared my worker." Zachary couldn't look up at Xuan. "I'm sorry, bud."

"It's okay, but while we were chatting, you fell asleep saying something. What's happening to us?"

"I don't know where to even start, Xuan?" Zachary covered his face, plopping on the couch.

"Tim and I had a secret business involving gold. Tim had his own venture in the auction business, so this was a little extra on the side. We didn't mean to invest much, but as time went on, we were forced to." Xuan got up and brought Zach a glass of water.

"I stopped paying my share for a few months and the business failed." Zachary then began to cry.

"So what happened after that, Zach?"

"We borrowed from a loan shark, and now Tim's gone, they are after me."

"So they're following you?" Xuan wasn't sold on Zachary's story.

"Are you fucking kidding me? Of course, they are. They chased me around town yesterday. I'm lucky I survived."

"So, what to do now, Zach?" Xuan was worried the men might finish Zachary before he did. "Are they professionals?"

"I don't know, Xuan. I need your help."

"Tell me more about these people."

CHAPTER FOUR

The rain was pouring and Xuan was in downtown Houston with Zachary. They were pushed back and forth on the crowded sidewalks as they searched for a building that Zach said belonged to the loan sharks.

"This is it, Xuan."

Who would've thought Xuan Lang would be helping his enemy?

"What are we waiting for? Go inside." Zachary walked up the long set of steps as Xuan's heartbeat was racing.

"Should we go in, or wait for him to come out?"

Xuan couldn't believe how inexperienced Zach was. Xuan tapped on the door and no one answered, so he went in and Zach trailed behind. Down the long corridor, every door had numbers and letters with no names written.

"Now what?" whispered Zachary.

"Are we in the right building?"

"Number Seven A." Zachary spotted the door afar. "In our contract, they wrote this room as the address"

Xuan hurried to the door, tapping hard. While they waited, Zachary bit his fingernails.

"Come in." They went inside. There was a mahogany desk and with an older man in a cowboy hat seated.

"Good afternoon, Sir," expressed Zachary. The man stared while Xuan didn't say anything.

"May I help you?"

"I'm Zachary Hamilton. I'm sure you're familiar with my late partner, Tim Marshall."

Xuan interrupted, "Let's cut to the chase. Tim Marshall and my friend here took a loan from you and it seems you're making a mistake by taking it out on my friend here."

"My name is William Sage and it's a pleasure to meet you, now you may sit." William ignored Xuan. Zachary sat playing with his fingers and Xuan looked on.

"Sadly, I'm aware of Tim's death but your friend,

Zachary was his business partner. It's suitable to say Zachary must pay off his debts." William rested his arms on the desk staring at Xuan.

"I'm struggling now. My wife just got fired, and we're only surviving on my retirement," pleaded Zachary. Xuan kicked Zachary which him off guard. Xuan thought he was giving this man too much information.

"You're in debt, Mr. Zachary. Am I not clear when I say you must pay me back?" William was becoming annoyed while Xuan kept his cool.

"I know but all I need is a favor."

"What is it? I'm not in the business of giving favors," sighed William.

"I need more time. At least six months."

"Are you fucking insane?" William stood up and hit the desk. It was a sight worth seeing as the man looked like he was having a temper tantrum. "You better have my money on this desk in two months, Hamilton, or else I will send you my boys over to give you a pleasant going-away party." William pulled a pistol out of his drawer and placed it in front of him.

"That will certainly do, Mr. Sage. Thank you," Xuan excused himself while pulling Zachary.

Xuan didn't care except he should be the one to

kill Zach. Zachary's debt wouldn't matter because he would be gone off the Earth before the deadline.

"It looked like I was the one doing all the negotiating and saved your life," said Xuan.

"You don't know, William. Tim used to tell me bad things about the guy."

"Like?" Xuan was speeding up to Zachary who was petrified.

"Not only did William take the life of someone who owed him, but he also destroyed the man's family by suing him afterward. Now, they are all living on the streets in the fucking ghetto. The wife is a crackhead and his children has been in and out of foster care."

"So, William Sage is the devil," grinned Xuan.

"The devil himself has a better face. I really hope Tim's now resting in heaven."

Xuan almost choked, hearing him.' "I hope you're right, Zach," said the old man sneeringly.

Xuan didn't have an exact plan on how to kill Zach, but he'll do it in joy. The old man turned on the radio to listen to the news hearing the weather report in the coming days. Xuan's isolation drained his spirits; seeing his daughter and wife running around the kitchen making his favorite dish.

Only if he'd stay home that day; it was the

mistake that changed his life forever. The Americans were going back to their country that day, but seven cowards showed up to his home and came across his wife and daughter preparing him dinner. They were having fun with their corpses when they dumped into the basement like old rags. The horrifying sight of their dismembered bodies haunted Xuan by the day.

———

The Banh Mi was almost ready as Xuan snapped out of thoughts. He pondered whether to call Katherine and Ethan over. When he decided to do so, the door-bell rang. Messy, he opened it and it was Ethan, frightened.

"What's wrong?"

"There's a woman at the shop, going crazy, throwing stuff all around." The young man was breathing as if he ran for his life. Xuan listened real-izing he still was dressed in his bedrobe but didn't care.

As they got closer to the shop, they heard Anna, Tim's wife cursing. "Oh my God! She knows," con-ceived Xuan.

"Go home, Ethan. I'll deal with this woman. Her

husband just passed away," Xuan patted Ethan and entered the shop.

"You!" Anna rushed towards Xuan, hitting him. "You killed Tim. You fucking bastard!"

"Calm down, woman." Xuan held her wrists tightly. It was the least he could do. "Your husband is one of seven responsible for the deaths of my wife and daughter."

Anna took a few steps back, looking at Xuan.

"What, what do you fucking mean?"

"Tim with six other Marines raped my wife and daughter and burnt their bodies. They tossed the corpses in my basement in Vietnam."

"No, no. Why would my Tim do that? You're lying. My Tim wouldn't do such a thing. Oh, God!"

"They did it, Anna. Many Americans have done bad things to our people." Xuan sat facing Anna. "Believe me, Anna. I have no choice."

"I should report you to the fucking police."

"You wouldn't do that, because it would mean I'd have to get rid of you, too. You know I could have set you up when you left Tim that evening. Instead, I had to hear his fucking sob story all night."

Anna was baffled and didn't move an inch. "So what's your plan now?"

"Wouldn't you want to know?" Xuan circled her, not yet giving her the pleasure of emotion.

She gulped, watching him, scared for her life.

Xuan kept staring and stayed silent.

"Then, I'll keep this our little secret under one condition," said Anna.

"I'm listening." Anna cleared her throat.

"You need to tell me, what other businesses Tim had. I need some money fast."

"I may consider it."

———

After Anna left, Xuan went directly to Katherine's house, to make sure Ethan was okay. Katherine was surprised to see Xuan in his robe and invited him in.

"I'm sorry to bother you, Katherine but I came by to tell Ethan I took care of our little problem at the shop."

Ethan suddenly came as Xuan was speaking.

"No worries, I took care of the problem. An old friend who's husband passed away. She needed some money and is possibly on drugs."

"May I get you a cup of tea?" asked Katherine.

"One cup wouldn't harm." Xuan sat as Ethan came, too.

"So who was that woman?" asked Ethan.

"A homeless person looking for food now that her husband had passed away."

"We should have called the police."

"I agree, but it's too late now. The woman is gone." Xuan looked down at his feet as he spoke.

"It's a shame we don't have a security camera," said Ethan.

"I'll get one from Highlands," smiled Xuan promising it wouldn't happen again.

"Tomorrow is my day off, but I'll come by to fix the mess she made."

"No need, Ethan. I'll clean it up."

"No offense, Xuan but I think you'll be tired after moving the second box," chuckled Ethan.

"Ethan! Watch your mouth," yelled Katherine from the kitchen.

"Maybe you're right, but I'll manage."

Katherine entered the room with two cups of tea and set it down. Xuan thanked her. "You've done well, Katherine."

"Glad you like it," smiled Katherine.

"I've been craving for some good tea."

"Ethan doesn't like it, but I drink it every morning." She took a sip not breaking eye contact. Katherine was attractive, but Xuan couldn't see her more than a friend. Even after his wife's death, Xuan was faithful even if it meant being alone for the rest of his life. His wife's memory would never be forgotten.

No one bothered to visit Xuan except Katherine and Ethan. Maybe they feared him. In the War, many Houston residents had lost relatives. Xuan knew this but he lost more than them.

"I'm afraid I have to go. My friends are waiting for me at the diner," said Ethan.

"I'll be leaving as well. My meal has probably overcooked." Xuan got up, smiling.

"No need to leave, Xuan. This is your home, too."

"Maybe some other time. I promise."

Ethan and Xuan left out together and Xuan's Banh Mi had overcooked, so he threw it away. When he finished cleaning, his phone rang.

"Let's meet tomorrow, Xuan." It was Zachary. "We'll be at the Crown Restaurant around noon." Zachary's tone was dispirited.

"I'm not sure if I'll be able to make it." He didn't want to meet with them yet and needed time to plan his second kill.

"You need to be here. Joshua will be coming too."

"I'll think about it. I don't understand why it's important. We're still grieving over Tim."

"Well, it is about Tim's death. We've hired a

private investigator to look into the matter. The police aren't doing their fucking jobs fast enough."

"Okay. Give me a minute, so I can get a pen."

"Lion Square, 10796 Bellaire Blvd. Not far from you."

"Thanks."

———

The alarm clock interrupted Xuan from a night full of pleasant dreams about his family. He got up and cooked some new Bánh mì. While doing so, the old man remembered the many pleasant mornings he spent back home. The radio was playing in the background discussing this weekend's town's county fair. Then the phone rang and it was Zachary. He wanted Xuan to accompany him to a local barbecue restaurant. Xuan told himself he would finish Zach off today once and for all.

"Hello?"

"Hey, bud. It's me, Zach." Xuan closed his eyes, trying not to curse.

"What happened now?"

"Joshua will help me."

"You told him about the loan shark?"

"Yeah. He's willing to help me out."

"Do you want to bring him into this?"

Zachary paused, considering saying something else.

"Look, let's talk about it at the restaurant."

"Ok."

"The Pit Room at noon. See you there, bud."

———

It was almost noon and Xuan got dressed. The old man grew tired, thinking about killing Zachary. This wasn't for a man his age. Xuan gathered some poisonous herbs and made a clear liquid. Xuan would poison Zach if he couldn't kill him with his knife.

The restaurant was nearby and the sun was blazing. Since the restaurant had reservations, Xuan waited until he was called. The place was packed for lunch.

"Hello, do you have a reservation, sir?" asked a gentleman.

Xuan panicked, afraid of holding up the line. "It should be under the name of Zachary Hamilton." The young man searched through a few pages of the reservation book while Xuan tapped his foot. "Here we go." Xuan was then invited inside and directed to Table 20. The restaurant's inside resembled a maze with the partitions separating the customers. Xuan followed the waiter and Zachary saw Xuan approaching. He stood up and embraced the old man.

"We've been waiting awhile for you." Zachary patted Xuan and led him inside to the table. They had already ordered and their plates was nearly empty. "Don't mind us. We were dead hungry and didn't know how late you'd be," said Zach, scratching the back of his head.

"Long time no see," said Joshua smiling while shaking Xuan's hand.

"I know. Where have you been all of this time, Joshua?"

"I went to Oklahoma on a business trip. It took longer than expected. I'm happy to be back. Too damn hot down there."

"I hear it's beautiful, though."

"Oklahomans live simple. It felt like I was living in England with the fucking Queen," laughed Joshua. "It was strange, the fucking women treat you like a king homesteading and shit. Big ass breasts and fucking rompers."

"We need to go," said Zachary.

A waiter came to the table, asking Xuan for his order. "A steak, rice and salad. And please bring me some red wine." The waiter jotted the order and asked, "How would you like your steak, sir?"

"Medium rare."

"That's a fucking pussy steak. You got to eat it rare, bud," said Joshua causing Zachary and the waiter to laugh.

"You're funny. But please give a steak - medium rare. Thank you."

The waiter nodded, leaving the area.

"I heard Zachary told you about what happened. It's a shame. Although I didn't know Tim well, he treated me well."

"Tim was a good friend. We served in Nam together. Great buddy. God rest his soul."

"Well, Joshua's in town to help an old buddy out, right?"

"Of course, I'll help as long as my friend here grants me a partnership in his company, I'll be glad to do so."

"So, you're setting stipulations?" asked Xuan.

"It's not quite a condition. My cash isn't even close to Tim's. There is no reason why I can't help an old friend." Joshua avoided looking at Xuan while eating.

"You'd take half of a poor man's assets, isn't that much to your advantage?"

Zachary stayed silent.

"Do you accept my offer, Zachary? Enough of this silly talk. This old man knows nothing."

Zachary stared at Xuan. "He's a long-time friend who only wants to help me, Xuan. Don't be so damn serious. We've been buddies since the old days back in Nam." Zachary winked at Joshua and Xuan just shook his head.

The waiter set Xuan's food down as the old man never experienced such luxury. As he ate, his mind shifted to executing his plan.

"When Joshua lends me the money, I can get rid of the loan shark once and for all."

"You shouldn't have gone to him in the first place. You are playing with your life."

"We had no choice, Xuan, and I didn't call you here to argue. We are grown-ups."

Xuan enjoyed the food, promising himself that he'd come here to eat again.

Then, the old man changed plans over his next target; making it Joshua. It wasn't the right time for Zach, so after eating, Xuan suddenly got up. "I'll be leaving, gentleman."

"So soon. It was a pleasure meeting you Xuan. Maybe, we'll see each other again," said Joshua, not looking.

"I'll be in touch, Zach."

Zachary shook hands, and Xuan left, not shaking Joshua's.

———

Xuan was back home doing laundry as his clothes had piled up for days. He mopped the basement floor and went upstairs, pulling out his favorite book "The Art of War" from the bookshelf. Xuan had read it many times, but every time he did, it felt like the first time. After reading a few chapters, the old man fell asleep with the book in his hands.

Xuan Lang had the same dream night after night; reminiscences of his daughter and wife with him at the beach, laughing. Binh was practicing swimming with her father while the ocean's waves vibrated. His wife, Phuong was preparing sandwiches underneath a rainbow umbrella. It was a classic moment Xuan will never forget.

An hour later, the old man awoke, sweating. The dream always ended with him losing them. Xuan's wailings echoed throughout the house. This pain left a lasting hole in his heart. He got out of bed, splashing water on his face but couldn't wash away the thoughts. He went downstairs and took some herbs from the cupboard. The suspense was becoming worse than the day of his family's funeral.

Ethan was alone working for the last few days, so Xuan went by to check on him. Before going, he made the young man a sandwich.

"I've been worried about you." Ethan pulled out a chair for Xuan.

"I've been very busy for the last few days. Hopefully, I can make it up." Xuan pulled out the sandwich and Ethan's eyes lit up.

"How are things going?"

"Not well, only a few customers came." As Ethan ate, the scene reminded Xuan of his daughter craving for a snack in the middle of the night.

"As you were. I'll be in the storage room checking inventory." He went over the logs from the last few days and everything matched up. Ethan was a very responsible young adult.

A customer came in causing Xuan to halt. He overheard Ethan interacting with the customer.

"Hello, sir. How may I help you?"

"Do you have chamomile?"

Xuan heard a bit of shuffling. "Yes, we do. Just a moment, please."

"Here you are," said Ethan wrapping the herbs neatly. "That will be two dollars, sir."

Xuan thought about leaving him the store once his mission was accomplished.

"Sir, it's almost eight. Should we close for the evening?"

Ethan caught Xuan reading the newspaper, not paying attention. "Oh, sure Ethan, you can go. I'll close. Thank you. You've done great."

"You look tired. I'm here to help, you know."

"Your mother will worry. We don't want her to, do we?"

"Okay, I'll be in first thing in the morning." Ethan walked out and Xuan followed him.

"Take the day off. It's Sunday. I don't think we'll have a lot of customers."

———

It was nightfall and the streets were empty. At his doorsteps, the old man saw his right window open. Xuan knew something was wrong because he never opened them ever. He opened the door quietly, taking his pistol from the flowerpot. There was a loud crash upstairs and Xuan knew someone was inside.

Xuan crept up the stairs. His heart was racing

more when approached his bedroom door sighting a man in a suit. It was Zachary rummaging through his drawers and Xuan couldn't believe what he was witnessing.

"What are you doing here?" Xuan spoke, holding his Baretta. Zachary stopped, getting up slowly.

"I can explain, Xuan it's not what you imagine."

"You killed them!"

"Killed who?"

"My wife and daughter."

"Listen, Xuan, I can explain." Xuan didn't have time for excuses. He aimed at Zachary's head.

"What did you say to my wife while you were raping her?"

Zachary backed up with his hands up. "I, I—".

"You have brought them hell in this life. Now, I'll make you a hundred times more."

Xuan twisted the silencer on the nuzzle but it wasn't the right size. Zachary's sweat was pouring down his face and Xuan was enjoying every second of his despair.

"Please don't kill me Xuan, I can help you."

"Do you think I'm here on vacation?" Xuan spat in Zach's face. "I've been following all of you for years; pursuing every last one of your feeble steps."

Xuan pressed the pistol to Zach's forehead, causing him to wince.

"Why are you here inside my house, you fucking bastard?"

"Joshua wanted to know more about you. Please, I didn't want to. If you let me go, I promise you'll never see me again."

Xuan stared at how pathetic Zachary seemed.

"By the way, say hi to Tim, will you? I'm sure you'll spend some time together in hell." Xuan shot Tim in the forehead, watching his body hit the ground. As much as it appeared psychotic, the old man enjoyed it. Xuan then dragged the body to the basement. He was mopping up the blood when someone had knocked.

"I'm coming!" shouted Xuan as he closed the basement door. His shirt covered in blood and he yanked it off. The knocks became noisier.

"Just a minute!" He examined to see if any blood was left. Then, the old man opened the door observing Katherine, Ethan, and another next-door-neighbor.

"We heard a gunshot from your house! Are you okay?" said Katherine.

"Oh! Yeah, I was cleaning out my gun, and it fired accidentally."

"Do you have a license, sir?" said the woman behind Ethan and Katherine, scrunching.

"I do. I'm not a criminal, ma'am. Ask my associates, Katherine and Ethan."

"Yeah, he's good, Maribel."

"I hope you're okay. I'd be scared to death. You could have killed yourself," said Katherine.

"I'm sorry to disturb you. I'll let an expert do my gun cleaning from now on."

"Ok, Xuan. Have a good night."

Katherine, Ethan, and Maribel left and Xuan closed the door, returning to his bedroom. The blood on the carpet wasn't easy to clean up. It took almost two hours of scrubbing to remove the stains.

Xuan had to get Zach's body out of the house. He decided to dump it at a nearby hill during the night. He cut up Zachary's body and bagged up the body parts. Quietly, the old man waited for the right time to dispose of the remains.

CHAPTER FIVE

Zachary's funeral procession was dull and Xuan was forced to go in order to conceal his motive. During the sea of continuous tears and hymns, Xuan felt lightheaded. He tried to avoid meeting with Zach's family members.

Xuan dumped Zach's body in the river instead of the hill because of dogs barking. Two days following, the body was found and there are still no suspects. As Xuan stood alongside Joshua Warren and Matthew Jones, Matthew kept chatting and didn't seem saddened by the news.

"Zachary was a great man. It's a shame he had to go like this," said Matthew.

"God takes the best from us. Rest in peace, bud," added Joshua bowing.

Xuan breathed as Zachary's wife approached.

"Will you be joining us for dinner?" she asked, teary-eyed.

"I'll be there." Xuan smiled, weakly. Zachary's two sons were alongside her, holding her tightly. Ben, Ronald, and Duong were having a chat with some of Zachary's old friends from the Marines and Xuan walked over.

"Gentlemen."

"Xuan Lang, it's been a while," said Duong, raising his drink.

"Drinking at a funeral? Talk about class," reflected Xuan. "It's unfortunate seeing one another on such circumstances."

Xuan perceived Ben, Ronald and Duong weren't close to Zachary, inferring from their unfriendly expressions.

"It's such a tragedy; no one deserves such a horrific end. Nobody deserves to die, period," said Duong.

"He was a kind-hearted man even when people cheating him," said Ben.

"It's a shame," replied Xuan.

"The man was up the ass in debt. I heard he was partners with Tim in the fishing business," said Ronald.

"Such gossip," said Xuan, looking at Joshua. They knew the truth.

They left to the reception to get food and offer their condolences. Zachary's sons came over to the table asking if they needed something. The men waved "no" and proceeded on chatting. Xuan saw they were talking business and wasn't interested. The old man then excused himself.

Meanwhile, Joshua Warren walked towards the bar and Xuan sat next to him.

"What are we drinking today?"

"You wanted this to happen, didn't you?"

"What do you mean?"

"How was Zach murdered after telling you everything?"

Xuan ignored, requesting a drink.

"I'll find out everything on you, Xuan Lang. There's some fishy about you being here."

That was the wrong thing to say. "Shall I also expose you and your army friends for the horrific murders and rapes in Vietnam?"

Joshua was bewildered. His face became blue knowing the old man kenned their darkest secret.

"I know everything, you fucking bastard. And after your drink, I'd advise you to get out of here before everyone here knows." Xuan smiled as the waiter came.

"Hurry up; your clock is ticking," chuckled Xuan, getting up after finishing his drink. Joshua got up quickly and walked.

"What are you going to do?" questioned Joshua when they reached the parking lot; feet away from Joshua's vehicle.

"I think you and I know what's next." Xuan pulled out his Baretta and pointed signalling Joshua to get inside. Joshua started the engine, driving off.

"It's such a shame we won't have a chance to say goodbye to Miranda." She was Joshua's wife, and because of her addiction, she was told to stay home.

"My friends will see I'm missing and will fucking kill you. You fucking Chink bastard."

"Shut the fuck up and drive. Don't stop until we reach the Fred Hartman Bridge. It's a nice day for swimming, huh!"

Joshua tried slowing down. "Keep driving and don't even think about doing anything stupid. I know where your family lives," said Xuan pressing the barrel to the side of Joshua's head.

"You didn't think this through. Did you?"

Xuan chuckled. When they reached the bottom of

the bridge, Xuan told Joshua to get out and turn off the engine. Xuan instructed Joshua to get on the pavement. "You'll fucking pay for this, you fucking chink bastard."

"Never once will I feel regret." Xuan spat in Joshua's face. "Climb over and I will not repeat."

Joshua looked around, trying to signal for anyone to help. It was dark and the cars kept going across.

"Nobody will help you, Josh. This is it."

Joshua climbed over the rail onto the bridge's platform. The view below was horrifying; large rocks and a flowing river.

"Your buddies are waiting for you in hell. Have fun." Xuan poked Joshua in the back with the gun and told him "Jump."

With one look, Joshua jumped to his death. Xuan gazed at his body while it crashed on the rocks into the water.

———

Xuan didn't return home. He decided it was time to head to Ben's house in Joshua's car minutes away. Ben came home right after the funeral and his wife and children were out front barbecuing. Xuan loosened his tie and walked through the family's front garden.

"Xuan?" said Ben squinting. Ben's wife escorted their children inside with their aunt.

"Hello, Ben. I'm sorry to interrupt, but our friend, Joshua is missing. I don't know where. He mentioned a lake."

"Oh, my! What happened?" His wife cut in.

"Joshua felt drained after the funeral and was driving me home. He stopped and when I went to pee, I came back and he wasn't there."

"We need to call the police right away," said Ben lowering the spatula after turning over burgers.

"I think he may be out there roaming around."

Ben's wife ran to call the police but had no idea how to describe. She told her sister to watch the kids while she, Ben and Xuan go out to find Joshua. Ben and his wife jumped in Joshua's car with Xuan in the passenger seat. They kept driving to the wrong areas, and after hours of searching, they stopped on the roadside.

"Why would Joshua leave you? This is kind of strange." Ben and his wife kept asking.

"Before I left the car, he was saying he was tired of life. I thought he was joking."

They drove off again and minutes later, reached a lake that Xuan said resembled the place they stopped at. They searched with their flashlights, calling his name and he was nowhere to be found.

On the way back, the couple told Xuan their life story; how and where they first met and when they bought their first home and had children. Xuan wasn't interested, just making small talk here and there. Ben told Xuan to come inside for coffee in the couple's living room.

"Bethany and Lucas are lovely kids, but I think we'll let their tutors go because we can't afford them any longer. Tutors are getting more expensive." Xuan listened to Andrea's non-stop chattering and wanted to fall asleep. They waited hoping to receive good news about Joshua while Xuan only wanted to kill Ben but couldn't.

"They won't need a tutor. You'll see they'll be top of their classes. Just keep them focused," said Xuan. Any minute, the police would be on their way. Sadly, the old man had to stick around.

"Let's hope so." She took a long sip, and then Ben joined them. "These sheriffs are taking long. It's almost midnight," said Joshua after talking with the police for the third time in hours. Ben lived in a rural town outside of Houston and the police said they were on their way.

"What are you over there talking about?" Joshua sat down next to Andrea, holding her hand.

"Bethany and Lucas, of course, honey."

"Those little rascals." Ben and Andrea laughed while Xuan smiled. He gave them privacy; turning away when they kissed.

Forty-five minutes passed and Xuan said, "I think I'll be heading home soon. I live rather far from here. The police are taking us serious, so I'll leave you my number just in case." As Xuan was getting up, the sheriff's car lights flashed outside.

Xuan, Ben, and Andrea walked out on the porch, greeting them.

"Good evening," said a fat sheriff. He tipped his hat and proceeded to say, "I'm sorry, but your friend, Joshua Warren appears to have taken his life."

The couple and Xuan gasped.

"What!?" replied Ben.

"Where?" asked Xuan.

"Down the Old Lakewood Pond next to the Fred Hartman Bridge. It's not deep, but the cliffs below it are deadly. It appears he jumped. We have some questions for you since you were the last one to see him."

"No problem, officer. I'm willing to help."

"Why would he do this? He was such a happy

man." Andrea clung onto Ben and didn't want to let go.

The sheriffs interviewed Xuan and then told him it was all they needed.

As they were leaving, they offered their deepest sympathies.

"VIETNAM WAR HERO, JOSHUA WARREN COMMITS SUICIDE"

The old man laughed as he read the front headline. His smile disappeared when he read through the article and spotted, *"Case is still under investigation for potential witnesses."*

"What witnesses?" yelled Xuan tossing the paper. "What does a man in grief have to do to get some recognition?"

Xuan knew he had to move on. The last time he saw Ben was the night of Joshua's disappearance a week ago, and it was time to kill him. No one knew of these men's past wrongs and Xuan hated that they were seen as hometown heroes. He vowed to expose them for what they have done even if it meant taking his own life.

Xuan was eating, thinking about how to proceed with Ben. It had to be quick. When he was nearly finished eating, someone gently knocked.

The old man was confused, placing his dishes in the sink. He then opened the door and it was Anna, Tim's widow.

"What are you doing here?" He looked around, afraid if anyone had seen her come.

"I read about your other victim, Zachary Hamilton. How clever you are!" She brushed past and walked inside. Not wasting time, she got comfortable, plopping next to his food.

"Who's next?" Anna grabbed the newspaper and read the headline — VIETNAM WAR HERO, JOSHUA WARREN COMMITS SUICIDE—. Xuan shushed her and yanked it from her, setting it on the countertop.

"Isn't that a lie?" snickered Anna.

"You have no business here."

"You're wrong about that, Mr. Killer. I do because you killed my fucking husband." Anna took out red lipstick from her handbag.

"What do you want from me?"

Anna took her time answering, putting it on while staring in her pocket mirror.

"Ten grand." She closed the mirror, waiting for the old man's response.

"You're fucking crazy. You have to go." He picked up Anna's handbag and pushed her towards the door.

"How nice of you to send me directly to the police station. Isn't it?"

Xuan moved in front of her. "You wouldn't dare."

"If you give me ten grand, I won't. I know you have money. All you fucking Chinks do." Anna tapped her foot, indicating she didn't have much time. "Give me the money and you can have Tim's cabin in Austin. I'm leaving town and don't need it."

Xuan looked at her, disgusted he was being bribed. He went upstairs to his safe and placed the money in a paper bag. When he came back down, he tossed the bag to Anna.

"It's all there. You can count it at home, but it's time for you to go. I have work to do." Xuan opened the door, not giving Anna satisfaction.

"As you were. Have a nice life, Xuan and remember what goes around, comes around." Anna handing Xuan the keys to the cabin and left.

Xuan picked up Ben's number off the kitchen

counter. He needed a plot to get him over. He told Ben he wanted to rehabilitate a cabin given to him. Since Ben renovated homes, the old man told him the money would be good if he can help.

———

Ben Rogers came alone. Little did he know, he was taking a trip to his grave. Xuan got his gear ready and left extra fuel in his car. His plan was for them to stay at the cabin for the day and at night, he'd make his move and burn the place down.

Xuan hadn't heard from Katherine or Ethan in days. When he was about to stop by the shop, Ben pulled up to the front of the house, beeping his horn. "Xuan!"

"Coming!" Xuan grabbed his duffle bag and left.

"Let's go fix em' up, bud!"

Ben drove for two hours in the woods to Tim's cabin. When they were driving, Xuan told Ben to look around. The beauty of wilderness struck Ben. It was relaxing and for at least a day, he'd be away from the constant noise of his two children.

"We're here," said Xuan when they arrived. They went inside, leaving their things on the porch.

"It's nice. We can do lots of things at this place. I can already see." snickered Ben, roaming around the cabin.

Xuan was left to carry the burden of this place for one day. Xuan only needed it for one reason; to get rid of Ben Rogers.

"I bought it when I first got to Texas. Do you like it?" Xuan cleaned off the table and unpacked the food he prepared.

"Who wouldn't like a place like this? It's so peaceful." Ben looked out of the window, captivated by the stunning landscape. Xuan opened two cans of cola while Ben wasn't looking and put a sleeping pill in one.

"You're right. Too bad! I don't have time to come out here more often. The fresh air could do me some good," said Xuan while taking a bite out from his sandwich. Ben sat down nearby, unwrapping his.

"This place is perfect for a picnic, and we are stuck with these--"

"Better something than nothing." Xuan gave Ben a can of cola.

"So, where shall we start?" asked Xuan.

"The front. As you can see, there are a few holes on the sides and the wind blows in at night."

"Next, change the boards. Maybe with oak with a touch of enamel. It would look amazing."

Xuan wasn't paying attention.

"The last thing is the kitchen. To be honest with you, Xuan, it looks like a shithole. If Andrea was here, she'd give it a good makeover."

"Give me a list of the things you need and I'll buy them."

"Will do. Plus, we'll be done in no time fixing this place up," Ben reassured. They went on talking about Tim, Zachary and Joshua and Xuan was getting restless, waiting for Ben to fall asleep.

After an hour, Ben started dozing off. Xuan waited a little longer before going to get the gas tank. "Ben?" The old man shook him to see if he was still conscious. "Ben?" The man was knocked out cold. Xuan got the tank out of the trunk and splashed it around the cabin. "Damn, I forgot the lighter." Xuan hurried back and found it in the glove department. Before burning the cabin, Xuan relived the moments he saw Ben, laughing with the others. He dropped the lighter, causing the cabin burst into flames. The old man watched as the cabin burned and its smoke was increasing. The old man pulled off, gratified that Ben Rodgers was on his way to Hell.

Ben's wife, Andrea was in shock by the unexpected death of her husband. She came to Xuan's house three days after the funeral.

"What will I do alone with these kids? They're broken by the loss of their father." Andrea cried constantly, sitting at Xuan's dining room table.

"You need to stay strong. Ben was an excellent man." Xuan placed a cup of tea in front of her.

"He should have asked you to come along. I don't know what he was doing out there alone."

"Zach had a cabin that Ben wanted to renovate, I heard. I wasn't feeling well, so I left him earlier. Ben said he had work to do out there."

"Terrible," grumbled Andrea as she cried not wanting to go away. The kids were at a neighbor's house. After Xuan had told her that the kids needed her at this very moment, Andrea finally decided to leave.

Xuan pulled out the files of his targets. Now that Tim, Zachary, Joshua, and Ben were all gone, it was time to focus on Matthew, Ronald, and for last, Duong Gian.

Xuan recognized his shop needed his keeping. On

the way there, he stopped at a park to clear his mind. The old man felt so mentally fatigued. Xuan looked at the families, spending time with one another. It was a sight he dearly missed.

The old man left and saw Katherine and Ethan inside the shop from out front. It was odd seeing her there, helping Ethan. Xuan greeted them and they looked up surprised.

"Long time no see, Xuan. Where have you been?" Katherine came over, embracing him.

"Here and there, visiting colleagues who recently passed," Katherine let go allowing Ethan to shake the old man's hand.

"We heard about the awful news."

"You must be feeling miserable. I'm so sorry." Ethan offered Xuan his seat.

"These were good buddies. It's sad to see them go."

"In better news, it's been a pleasure operating the store," continued Katherine.

"Our lives have been better since you moved here and offered me this job," said Ethan. "I get a chance to spend time with my mother and save money. Maybe I'll buy a Macintosh?"

"I'm glad to hear that young man. Even when I'm not here one day, you must help out your mother?"

Katherine and Ethan looked at each other. "Wait, does this mean you're leaving, Xuan?"

Xuan lowered his head. "No, not yet but one day."

Their stares made him feel awkward. Xuan couldn't reveal anything. If he did, he would have to kill them.

"Xuan, are you listening?" Katherine waved her hand.

"Sorry. What were you saying?"

"Where will you go?"

"Back to Vietnam. America is a beautiful but home is home."

"I'm sure your family misses you," said Ethan.

Xuan wasn't close to his relatives and grew distant after the shocking death of his two angels. "I'm sure they do."

As they were talking, Xuan hadn't noticed three men in front of the shop, looking around. They finally walked inside and Xuan stood up, surprised. It was Matthew, Ronald, and Duong.

"What are you fellows doing here?" said Xuan shaking their hands.

"Hello, Xuan. We have a few questions if it isn't too much trouble," said Duong looking at Ethan and Katherine who got his drift.

"Will you be okay, Xuan?" asked Katherine.

"It's fine. These gentlemen are close buddies. Give us a few minutes, please. Thank you."

Ethan and Katherine went to the back and Xuan turned his attention to them.

"To what do I owe the pleasure, gentleman?"

"We need some answers," added Matthew.

"Please, sit." Xuan pointed with only Duong sitting, keeping his eyes on Xuan.

"We don't want to waste time. You've been close to us and it seems to be a coincidence that our friends have died since you came," said Duong.

Xuan knew they had nothing. "It's strange, I agree. I even think someone is following me. That's why I have two workers at all times here. Who knows, maybe I'm next?"

"Do you have enemies here in America?" asked Matthew.

"Yes, a lot." thought Xuan. "None I know of."

"I moved here from the Philippines around two years ago and never had an argument. Why would someone want to kill an old guy like me? I'm someone's grandfather," joked Xuan causing the men to laugh.

"I don't know. Someone is out to kill us. It seems like every fucking week," expressed Ronald.

"You should stick together more often."

"You mean we should stick together." Matthew corrected Xuan.

"You need protection, Xuan. You're more helpless here than we are," replied Duong.

"Listen, I am grateful for your suggestions but I don't want to get caught up in this. Maybe we can talk about this another time."

"You don't want to hear about it. Well, me too. Fuck it. Let's celebrate life tonight," said Ronald.

To life then!" said Matthew clearing his throat while crossing his arms.

"We'll be having dinner. Every month, we have these dinner gatherings and tonight you're invited".

"Ok, just write down the address."

As Matthew was writing, Xuan pondered which of the men would be his next victim. Not Duong, the Vietnamese traitor would save him for last. He portrayed himself as the leader and deserved a heinous ending.

Matthew was full of himself but was the most honest out the bunch.

Ronald was arrogant, flaunting his wealth to no end. No one wouldn't miss him if he was taken out.

The three men left and Xuan noticed Katherine and Ethan also had left. They deserved some time off and Xuan called, telling them he had an important dinner to go to and to take the rest of the day off.

Xuan closed the shop and went home to pick out his best suit for the occasion.

CHAPTER SEVEN

"This way, Sir." A waitress led Xuan through the crowded restaurant packed with rich kids and parents. Xuan assumed Duong chose it because of its white-bread atmosphere.

"Thank you." Xuan reached where Matthew, Ronald, and Duong were seated.

"Glad you could make it, Xuan." smiled Matthew, telling the old man to sit.

"This place is packed, isn't it?"

"This has become our favorite restaurant. It's one of Houston's most celebrated among the youngsters as you can see," added Duong, calling over a waiter.

Xuan looked around, seeing what appeared to be horseplay. "Did you guys order already?"

"No, we waited for you this time," said Ronald.

"So Xuan, tell us about that cabin in the woods," started Duong.

Xuan took his time, answering. "Honestly, Tim was going to sell it to me, but we couldn't close the deal."

"Such a shame it burned to pieces." Duong looked at Xuan as if he knew something.

"If Tim was kind enough to sell it to you, he must have trusted you'd do good with it. He always told me it wasn't for sale," added Matthew.

"Wow, really? Anna had dreams of designing that old thing. By the way, where is she anyway?"

"Maybe she's fucking that young carpenter, Billy? That woman has always been a whore."

Everyone chuckled.

"I never met her, so I wouldn't know," continued Xuan.

The waiter put their food down and filled their glasses with beer.

"Do you have something to say Ronald?" asked Xuan disappointed with all the questioning. "Just keep playing the victim," conceived Xuan.

"Not at all, just curious how the cabin burned down by a simple fire. Ben doesn't doze off too long."

"I don't know," said Xuan.

"Then, it has to be Anna. No one else knew

besides her where the cabin was. But you were there before, right?"

"I don't remember exactly. Tim took me to a lot of places. Why are you insuiating I did something, Ronald?"

"Maybe it was an accident as they said," added Duong.

"Sorry, Xuan. I'm only looking at the situation, that's all. Don't take things personal."

Ronald couldn't stop staring at Xuan and Xuan noticed. He wasn't to take out all three at once and the old man couldn't let Ronald take the strings into his own hands even if it meant killing him tonight. Xuan's eyes slowly drifted to Ronald who was chewing like it was his last meal. Xuan deemed it such. Matthew and Duong were chatting while Xuan was planning his move on Ronald. It had to be done quickly, meaning right here, right now.

After a few beers, the guys chatted about business. Xuan brought a bottle of poisonous herbs made into liquid form, and it was his most deadly weapon. He ordered a bottle of champagne and Ronald finished his first glass in one swallow.

"We're going out for a smoke. We'll be back." Xuan felt like the Lord was on his side by sending Matthew and Duong away. Ronald was a heavy drinker but didn't smoke. Xuan offered him another glass as Ronald's eyes bobbed on a tall blonde with big breasts passing by. This was the perfect chance to get him.

"Go get her, Ron. She's looking at you. Look at those damn tits," said Xuan hyping Ron up.

"You don't have to say anything. I'm already getting up."

Xuan looked at how stupid this guy was. While Ronald was chatting, Xuan pulled out the liquid poison and dropped it all in Ronald's glass. Meantime, the blonde turned down Ronald, and he came back embarrassed. He blasted her while sipping on his drink.

Xuan observed Ronald and then excused himself. He waited next to the bar, watching him. For two minutes, Ronald was choking and then became unconsciousness, falling to the ground. A waiter yelled for help and the people in the restaurant started screaming. Duong and Matthew ran back inside as Xuan tried giving Ronald CPR. Ronald Ravens was dead.

Within minutes, the medics came to take the body out, and the police interviewed everyone. They then courted off the restaurant which was ordered to close.

"How did this happen? He was okay when we left." Matthew's quivering was the only thing heard in the empty restaurant.

"You should go back home, I'll talk with the police," insisted Xuan. Ronald and Matthew left while Xuan didn't wait around much longer. He grabbed a bottle of wine and rejoiced once he arrived home.

"Five down and two more to go," the old man thought as he pondered over the last victim. I could have killed all of them, but it would have made him look suspicious being the only person alive from the group. For the rest of the evening, Xuan cooked dinner enjoying a bowl of Pho. After finishing, he went to the basement and grabbed up a box.

There were many pictures of his family; all happy moments they spent together. He cherished the day he returned from the army and it was his birthday. Binh and Phoung made his favorite cake, along with some tasty Banh mì. Their smiles were priceless and he remembered them for ages.

Xuan then imagined about his return home. He'd be the only one alive. He shoved the pictures back in the box and kicked it under the kitchen table. Xuan's patience was running out but he knew it would be all over soon.

———

The following morning, Xuan got out of bed thinking about his next target, Matthew Jones. But there was one problem, he didn't have his address or phone number.

When he reached the kitchen, he heard the newspaper hitting the door. Xuan brought it inside, concentrating on the front page headline -- POSSIBLE SERIAL KILLER IN HOUSTON'S SUBURBS --. The old mand didn't see himself as such; he was only seeking revenge. If Xuan was in the army like his victims, the Americans would have given him a purple heart for killing the Gooks as they labeled them.

He set the paper down. "Damn reporters have nothing else to talk about." His whisper was loud enough to hear as he went to go shower.

"These old bones are kicking in," said Xuan as he put on his robe. He loved the mornings in Texas especially before people went to work. The old man looked out the window and saw Katherine and Ethan walking down the street with groceries. The young man's hand had a wrap on it and Katherine was struggling, carrying most of the bags. Xuan ran outside to help.

"Hand them to me," commanded Xuan as he approached. They were surprised to see the old man in his robe again.

"Xuan?"

"You should come over for breakfast. Mom's cooking bacon and eggs," said Ethan.

Xuan looked at Ethan's hand. "What happened, young man?"

"I was riding my bike and didn't notice the tire was flat. I fell off when I braked."

Xuan slightly grinned, praying they didn't hear about Ronald Raven's death. The borough was small enough that everyone knew even if a tire was stolen.

"You went shopping injured," joked Xuan.

"It's Mom's fault. We could have taken two trips or a taxi home," complained Ethan.

"Don't baby him; he isn't handicapped. That cut is smaller than a pinhole," remarked Katherine as they reached their steps.

"Let's go inside. I'll start breakfast."

Xuan's mind traveled back to happier times back home. "How could I say no to bacon and eggs?"

Xuan helped her set the groceries down and sat

next to Ethan. Just like the time when they first met officially. "So, Xuan. Did you decide on when you're leaving town yet?" asked Ethan.

"Yes, maybe soon. My house in Vietnam is now fixed up. A typhoon struck it a few months ago."

"Wow, I imagine it's beautiful in Vietnam. I've read many stories on the war and even saw Apocalypse Now."

"Ethan!" yelled Katherine.

"Ok, mom. Sorry!"

"My house has three rooms, a large kitchen like your mother's, and one big front room. It's not much, but we manage."

"You can start setting the table for your mother, Ethan," yelled Katherine from the kitchen.

Ethan began standing up but Xuan stopped him, putting his finger to his mouth. "Sit. I'll do it. Tell me where everything is."

Ethan pointed to the cupboard on the left and Xuan helped Ethan set the table before Katherine came in with the food. The three had a long chat about Ethan's living on campus. The young man got a four-year scholarship and Xuan was proud of him. The old man was glad they didn't mention the recent murders in the town.

Xuan excused him, recognizing he started caring about Ethan and his mother too much. This wasn't the old man's plan. When he unlocked his door, Matthew was inside sitting, looking at TV.

"Matthew?" Xuan gasped setting down the food Katherine had given him. "Hello, Xuan. I didn't mean to trespass but Duong's working today and I'm buying a new car. You're the only one I trust being around these days."

"How did you get in?"

"I knocked and turned the knob finding it unlocked. I hope you don't mind. We're buds, right?" Matthew scratched his head as he explained. "No problem. I wished you would have called first. You don't know whom I might have had in here." "Sorry, bud but are you up for a little drive?" said Matthew walking to the kitchen and pulling out a juice carton from the fridge.

"Sure, let me get dressed." Xuan looked at the box of photos under the table. He pretended to straighten things up, throwing a rag over it.

"I'll be right here."

There's was no time to waste as the perfect chance

came to kill Matthew. The old man devised a plan as he got dressed. "It must be my lucky day."

Xuan and Matthew rode for thirty minutes to the Helfman Ford dealership. As they drove through the hot sun, Matthew blasted country music and Xuan tried blocking out the sound. When he spoke, Matthew lowered the volume.

"I like this car, to be honest. How much did it cost you?" asked Xuan, looking out the window.

"Not much." Matthew made a U-turn. "What do you want to get now?"

"Maybe a Ford Pinto."

Matthew nodded and Xuan was thinking about his plan. If they went out for a test drive, he could poison him; causing the car to drive off a cliff. Xuan smiled imaging as they pulled up in the car lot.

Matthew talked with a salesman while Xuan walked around checking out the cars. Some were so expensive that he believed no one would ever buy them.

Matthew was fixated on buying the Ford Pinto, and the salesman offered him to go on a test drive. Xuan got in first and Matthew slowly drove off. Xuan just needed to get Mattew unconscious. "Damn, I left the beers back home. What to do?" realized the old man. He looked down seeing there was a fire extinguisher underneath.

Once they reached an isolated area, Xuan spoke. "Matthew, I think the back tire is losing air" The car came to a sudden halt, and Matthew turned to him.

"Are you fucking serious?"

Matthew jumped out and slammed the door. He walked to the back and inspected it.

"Is it this one?" He got on his knees, sharply observing it.

"Yeah, that one." Xuan unlocked the fire extinguisher and got out, seeing Matthew bent down.

"Are you sure it's this one, I don't see anything wrong with it?" Matthew was about to get up and Xuan hit him in the back of the head. Matthew laid on the ground stretched out but was still conscious.

Xuan dragged him and put him in the passenger seat. He drove away, stepping on the gas with full force. The old man drove until he reached a mountain range a few miles down the road. He pulled Matthew's body over to the driver's seat and strapped his seatbelt. Then, he got out and pushed it towards the end of a cliff with all his force. When it reached the edge, it got stuck but after pushing it harder; the car flipped over and fell to its end, causing a big explosion.

As Xuan walked down the road, he was lucky someone spotted him in an old pickup truck. "Are you okay mate?"

"I'm lost. My car broke down some miles down. The engine died."

The man tried chatting, but Xuan told him he didn't speak English well. The man told him he was from Alabama and here working in Houston. As they drove, the man cursed complaining about traffic.

"Thank you," said Xuan when he reached his shop. The man saluted him, saying they could hook up in the evenings at a bar a few miles away. Xuan knew he'd never see him again. Once home, he listened to a message from Duong on his answering machine. The old man knew time was ticking as he edged closer to ending his misery.

CHAPTER EIGHT

Xuan spent the next few days home. Duong left messages on Xuan's answering machine indicating he was on the verge of committing suicide. The police found Matthew's body charred so badly they couldn't do an autopsy. The dealership wanted payment for the car from Ronald's girlfriend and the news coverage on the ordeal was on every TV set in the town.

Xuan didn't see Katherine nor Ethan before they left for a family vacation. It was good they'd taken off because Xuan was close to ending his mission and they'd never see him again. Once, Katherine told Xuan about the murder of her first husband five years ago while he was on a business trip in Peru. Ethan was young and Katherine felt lonely until she met her current husband, whom she had a stepson but the man was always away working. That son stayed with the father's mother and only came by a few times a year. Katherine focused more on Ethan than her husband. Xuan was surprised she moved on so quickly and didn't seek revenge. He couldn't close his eyes at night in peace knowing his family's killers were still alive breathing.

Xuan thought deeply about his homeland during this time off. The food is impeccable and the best meals were on the streets - sitting on little plastic stools in the marketplaces. The food stands were open 24 hours and people of all ages would enjoy. Seafood was Xuan's favorite. He remembered a time when he would come close to the stove, while his wife Phoung was cooking and try to sneak a bite. She'd smack his hand and they'd laugh.

The phone rang and it snapped Xuan out of his daydream.

"Hello?"

"It's me, Duong."

Xuan cleared his throat. "Yes, I know."

"Why haven't you returned my calls. I'm fucking stressed."

"I've been busy with the shop. My workers have gone on vacation."

"Ok. I just wanted to let you know the neighborhood is having a veterans parade in about two hours. I hope you'll come and hear me speak."

"Sure, I'll be there. Where?"

"St. Greenwood. Everyone will be there. Don't worry! No one will try to kill us there."

"Then, I'll be there."

Xuan hung up and went to his bedroom picking out a suit. It was almost five and at six, the parade was beginning. He took a peek out the window and saw neighbors walking already towards the parade. Xuan would listen to his speech and execute his plan on Duong later in the evening. The old man was thankful Ethan and Katherine were out of town.

———

It was 6 o'clock and Xuan left for the Parade. He followed seeing families were cheering and waving flags at the soldiers and band members. Xuan hated them all except those who defended freedom. He had the highest respect for anyone in the military being a former soldier himself. Walking through the crowd, he felt out of place. The old man knew his retaliation wouldn't happen here; there were too many people around.

The troops stood, waiting for the orders of their general to salute. Everyone crowded the stage area till Duong Dian appeared; carrying his address.

Duong came out minutes later, opening his paper to speak.

"Ladies and Gentleman. Thank you for coming out this evening. In the past few months, I've lost so much as I did in Nam. I saw life in its purest form taken away, and as destiny proves repeatedly, it can be relentless at times."

Xuan scrunched.

"My fellow soldiers, soulmates, friends and most importantly, brothers who lost their lives in defending liberty."

The crowd clapped and Xuan wanted to leave.

"God blessed me, five years ago when we, the seven men from Houston, were on their way to Nam to serve this country gracefully." Duong paused, gathering himself.

"Within the last few weeks, I feel defeated. Unfairly crushed by life, but it doesn't mean I'll stop fighting to bring justice! To put the one responsible behind bars for the rest of their pathetic life. There is no doubt there is one man behind all of this and I shall find him. I promise you."

The crowd cheered as Xuan was shocked. "Was that his cue that he knows?"

Duong was leaving and the old man left, not interested in seeing the soldiers march. As he was walking away, a voice shouted, "Xuan!" He kept walking and Duong ran towards him.

"That was a nice speech. Little shorter than I expected, but it was satisfying."

"You thought it wouldn't be any good?" Why didn't you stay to watch the soldiers march?"

"You're younger than me, Duong. An old man like myself can't do too much activity. I'd invite you over for a drink, but you're busy campaigning," said Xuan.

"I'm free. I said what I needed. Honestly, I don't like watching these soldiers marching. It's ROTC stuff."

They laughed as Duong was choking.

"Easy, easy, my friend. I live five minutes away."

They chatted and Xuan came up with praises about Duong's speech. "I lured the rabbit into the trap, at last," conceived Xuan.

"This is beautiful," praised Duong when they reached his home. Xuan noticed Ethan and Katherine were back in town. What are they doing here? They were cleaning up. Xuan tried dodging them but Katherine saw Xuan.

"Xuan!"

Gasping, Xuan turned around. "Hey Katherine. You're back so early. I hope all is well" Katherine approached them in the garden.

"We actually went to visit my mother. We wanted to surprise her." She glanced at Duong. "Care to introduce me to your friend?" Katherine extended her hand out.

"This is Duong Gian, a Vietnam Vet."

Duong replied, "Nice to meet you, Madame."

"Katherine, may I invite you inside for a drink with my friend," proposed Xuan.

"Oh no, thank you. My pie's in the oven. Go on ahead."

"Nice to meet you again, Madame."

"You, too."

They went inside the house and Duong mentioned how cozy the place was.

"This reminds me of a family I once knew?" Duong sat as Xuan went close the door.

"I bought when I first laid eyes on it," Xuan said, taking off his coat.

"I'll get us some drinks." Xuan left not planning on poisoning Duong. He wanted the coward to suffer. The Vietnamese never should cross one another and he did.

Xuan brought two beers and Duong was stretched out on the couch with his eyes half-closed.

"You're tired already?" Xuan chuckled, handing him a beer.

"It's been a long day, filled with rehearsals. I didn't know the event was going to be that big."

———

The men chatted for hours and the clock showed 9 PM. Xuan was ready to go ahead with Duong's execution.

"Excuse me. I'll be back. I have to go to the bathroom."

"Ok."

Xuan went to the bedroom first, looking back to make sure Duong wasn't looking. Underneath the bed, he pulled out a rope he bought from the farmer's market for the occasion. He held it behind his back and close the bedroom door. When Xuan reached the bottom of the steps, he saw Duong with a photo in his hand. He gazed closer and saw it was from the box under the table. The box's lid was cast on the floor.

Duong chuckled. "These two women ring a bell. Don't they?" He said flicking the picture.

"What are you doing with that?"

"You killed my friends, didn't you?"

There was a long silence before they saw a butcher knife on the kitchen counter. They ran towards it, knocking each other down and the knife fell from the shaking.

"You bastard? I will kill you!"

Duong tried going for it, but Xuan hit him in the head with a frying pan and put the rope around his neck, dragging him backwards.

"I remember their last words. Their pleas for help, the cries. Oh! it sounded so good," Duong said as he struggled to get loose from the old man's grip.

"Your friends are rotting in hell and you will, too."

Duong was desperately gasping for air. He then elbowed Xuan in the stomach, causing the old man to release him. He raced to the knife but Xuan's pain didn't stop him. When Duong bent to grab it, Xuan kicked him into the cabinets. Duong's head slammed into the hardwood and Xuan kicked him with his old boots. Duong was alive but streams of blood were spewing from his mouth.

Holding him in a chokehold, Xuan grabbed the knife and slit his throat. "Burn in the pits of hell alongside your friends." Xuan then stabbed Duong three times. Feeling like it wasn't enough, he stabbed twenty more times; each blow saw blood gushing in all directions. Seeing Duong was gone, Xuan pushed Duong's body off of him and embraced the moment. The old man got up off the floor, someone knocked and then opened the door.

"I brought you some pie; Thought you'd like it." It was Katherine. "Oh, my god!" she yelled dropping the pie.

She looked at the knife in Xuan's hands, holding her mouth. The woman trembled not moving an inch.

"Xuan, what did you do!?"

Katherine then realized Xuan was probably the cold-blooded murderer the police was looking for.

"Please, Katherine. I can explain. This man was a rapist and killer." His bloody hands tried touching her, but she pulled back. Xuan knew she'd go to the police but he couldn't kill her.

"This coward raped and murdered my wife and daughter. I'm asking you not to say anything."

Katherine stared remembering she forgave the murderer of her husband but couldn't find the same sympathy for Xuan.

"You'll go to prison, killer! I don't believe you were around my son!" said Katherine, running out slamming the door shut.

"I'm so sorry, Katherine!"

Xuan rushed packing his suitcase after washing his bloody hands. The old man dashed out of the door, ignoring the pain in his stomach from the hit by Duong.

He put on a baseball cap and wandered through the night, knowing that his face was probably on the news already.

The nearest motel was one mile away, and Xuan knew he could only stay there for one night. People on the street passed by him and he looked down; his cap shielded his eyes.

When he found the place, there was a middle-aged woman waiting behind the reception desk. She lowered her glasses when Xuan came in.

"A room for one, please." Xuan looked behind to see if anyone was trailing him.

"ID and credit card, please."

Xuan handed her his passport and said he only had cash. The woman was popping chewing gum looking over the passport and then went to get the room keys. A few couples passed through the lobby causing Xuan to look away.

He remembered the box of photos he left behind. Nearly every memory will be defunct and lost forever. The receptionist came back. She handed Xuan the keys. "Have a lovely stay."

"Room 34." Xuan passed through the hallway and the room was at the very end. He had trouble unlocking it at first. When he opened the door, he found it full of dust.

"I see they didn't even bother cleaning it." Frustrated, Xuan set his suitcase on the floor and locked the door. He looked out the window. There was no one outside.

Xuan sat on the bed, defeated. His life was destroyed. He made one mistake of not locking the front door.

For two hours, he couldn't fall asleep weeping about what will happen now. Xuan believed his daughter and wife were disappointed since he got caught by Katherine.

"5 AM" showed the clock. The old man turned on the television and saw his image all plastered on the news with the headlines reading underneath: SERIAL KILLER IDENTIFIED - XUAN LANG

FROM VIETNAM - MANHUNT UNDERWAY. "Goddamit, Katherine," yelled Xuan as he watched. Law enforcement agencies from all over Texas were searching everywhere. They showed images of Xuan's passport photo and the ones with his family from the box. The words, "WANTED" was written underneath his. Neighbors who never spoke to Xuan now were on camera uttering their suspicions.

———

Xuan Lang regretted not killing Katherine. If it wasn't for his decency unlike his enemy, he would have done so. It was a problem that will haunt him for the hours to come.

Minutes later, as Xuan was closing his eyes, steps could be heard thundering outside the door. He knew what it meant. The old man got up off the bed and walked over to the corner where he placed his suitcase.

"Xuan Lang! Responsible for the deaths of seven US Marines. This is the FBI. Come out and put your hands on the back of your head where we can see them." Police lights were flashing outside and dozens of deputies were taking up positions in every direction. Xuan pondered being locked up for the rest of his life or the likelihood of martyrdom. "My fate is in my hands," shouted Xuan.

He took out the Baretta and loaded it with one bullet. The FBI begged for him to surrender, but they didn't hear anything. "Breach the fucking door." When they did, Xuan Lang ended his life being the last one to murder.

www.ingramcontent.com/pod-product-compliance
Lightning Source LLC
Chambersburg PA
CBHW030351200726

48286CB00013B/1086